PENGUIN YOUNG READERS LICENSES
An Imprint of Penguin Random House LLC

© 2017. All rights reserved.
HATCHIMALS™ is a trademark of Spin Master Ltd., used under license.
First published as *The Wishing Star Waterfall* in the United Kingdom in 2017 by Puffin Books.
Published in the United States in 2018 by Penguin Young Readers Licenses, an imprint of Penguin Random House LLC, 345 Hudson Street, New York, New York 10014.
Printed in the USA.

Written by Kay Woodward
Illustrated by Lea Wade

ISBN 9781524788216   10 9 8 7 6 5 4 3 2 1

HATCHIMALS™
THE FROZEN WISH

Penguin Young Readers Licenses
An Imprint of Penguin Random House

Contents

A Cloudy Day

"I *wish* we could go to the fireworks show tonight." Ava sighed. She was lying upside down on her bed, her hair spilling onto the carpet.

"*I* wish we could go to the backyard," Oliver said, looking out the window at the thick gray clouds blanketing the sky. "It's been ages since we last went to Hatchtopia, hasn't it, Duke?"

Duke zoomed over and landed on Oliver's shoulder, ruffling his hair.

Duke was Oliver's very own Hatchimal—a special creature from a world called Hatchtopia. Just a few weeks ago, Ava and Oliver had found two amazing speckled eggs in their backyard. They could hardly believe it when Duke and Pippi had hatched

from inside them!

Oliver had decided Duke was a Draggle, because he looked like a cross between a dragon and an eagle. Ava had decided Pippi was a Penguala, because she had a furry tummy like a koala and wings like a penguin's flippers. Ava and Oliver had raised their Hatchimals from babies all the way to kids, and already they felt as if they'd known the little creatures forever.

The Hatchimals were also the reason

A Cloudy Day

Ava and Oliver were so very desperate
to get out into the backyard. More than
anything, they wanted to step through
the secret door they had discovered
in their magnolia tree and visit
Hatchtopia again! But their parents
were away, and Aunt Sophie was in
charge. And, since their aunt thought
it looked like rain, Ava and Oliver had
been stuck inside the house *all day*. It
had been a very *long* day, too.

Duke hopped off Oliver's shoulder
and fluttered in front of him, making

The Frozen Wish

funny faces to cheer his friend up.

Duke's fur was a mixture of purple and white, and his beak was bright blue. His miniature wings were blue, too, and decorated with glossy purple scales. At that moment, they were beating so fast, they were almost invisible.

Oliver giggled. "Look at Duke!"

Ava flipped the right way up. "Oh no!" she gasped—but she wasn't looking at Duke. The wind from Duke's wings had reached the china model of the Statue of

Liberty that was on the desk nearby, and the figurine was wobbling. As Ava and Oliver watched, it began to fall as though in horrible slow motion toward the floor. The figurine was a souvenir from their parents' honeymoon in New York City. If it broke, they would be so upset.

Peowww!

A blur of pink fur shot across the room, and a little creature neatly caught the souvenir with one wing.

"Pippi, you star!" cried Ava.

The Frozen Wish

Ava's Hatchimal smiled shyly, and her eyes glowed sunshine yellow.

Pippi's fur was mostly pink, apart from the beautiful teal-colored fur around her eyes and on her tummy. Her feet were purple and her beak was pink. And, on top of her head, there was a tuft of fuzzy purple fur.

"What's all that noise?" called a voice.

"Uh-oh!" said Ava. "It's Aunt Sophie! We need to hide the Hatchimals!"

A Cloudy Day

They could hear Aunt Sophie's footsteps on the stairs. Pippi glided over to Ava, who hugged her tightly.

"It's fine!" Oliver said. "Mom and Dad think they're just toys, so why wouldn't Aunt Sophie believe that, too?"

"Ollie, you're a genius!" exclaimed Ava. She looked at the Hatchimals. "Did you hear that, guys? Pretend to be toys!"

The Frozen Wish

The Hatchimals' eyes brightened, and they nodded eagerly.

"That's right," said Oliver. He leaped to his feet and marched over to his desk. Quickly, he sat down and flipped open his math book. "Just act natural, like me."

The footsteps were right outside the bedroom door now.

"Here we go . . . ," whispered Ava, grabbing a book of her own.

The door swung open.

"There you are!" cried Aunt Sophie.

The Frozen Wish

She was dressed in flowery clothes, as usual, and her super-curly hair bounced merrily all around her face. "Didn't you hear me?" she said. Her eyes flicked between her niece and nephew. "Oliver, I don't for one minute believe you're doing homework. Ava, your book is upside down. So what *have* you both been up to all afternoon?"

Ava put her book down and smiled sheepishly. "We were playing with our toy Hatchimals, Aunt Sophie," she said. "Look! Mine's called Pippi."

"What sweet little toys!" said Aunt Sophie. She peered at Duke and Pippi curiously. "Why don't you show me how they work?"

Oliver pretended to press Duke's tummy. The little Draggle promptly hiccuped.

"Ta-daaaa!" said Oliver.

"Hic!" Duke hiccuped again.

"That's enough now, Duke," Oliver said under his breath.

But Duke really *did* have the hiccups.

He hiccuped a third time. And a fourth.

Aunt Sophie raised an eyebrow. "Is it going to make that noise all day? Perhaps you should take the batteries out—"

"NO!" shouted Ava, making everyone jump—including Duke. He blinked in alarm, then his eyes turned yellow and he gave a contented sigh.

"Phew!" Ava said. She had startled his hiccups away!

A Cloudy Day

"Excellent," said Aunt Sophie. She peered out the window as she stood up. "I think the weather's clearing up," she said. "You can probably play outside tomorrow."

She headed for the door, totally missing Oliver's victory dance behind her. "Now, what shall we do tonight?

The Frozen Wish

Shall we play a nice game of cards?"

Ava and Oliver exchanged glances. They'd played cards yesterday evening, too. Ava wasn't sure she could face another game!

Ava took a deep breath. "Aunt Sophie?" she said. "If the weather's better, could we maybe go and see the fireworks in town tonight? Please? I *love* fireworks."

Oliver gave her a thumbs-up.

"Sorry, sweetie, the fireworks display is far too late for you," Aunt Sophie

A Cloudy Day

said. "Anyway, it's so cloudy, you won't be able to see a thing!"

Ava's face fell, and when their aunt wasn't looking, Oliver tickled her in the ribs. "Remember we're going to Hatchtopia tomorrow," he whispered. "That's way better than *any* fireworks."

*

In bed that night, Ava tried very hard not to listen to the **pop, whizz,** and **bang** of the fireworks going off in town, but it was useless.

The Frozen Wish

They sounded amazing. All Ava could think about was how awesome the fireworks must look, and there was no way she could sleep. So she went looking for Pippi instead.

Ava found her whispering away with Duke under the desk. They stopped talking as soon as Ava appeared, but when she asked what

they'd been whispering about, Pippi
just shook her head.

"Nuh-uh. Surprise," said the
Penguala, her eyes twinkling.

*

The next morning, Ava and Oliver
waited nervously as Aunt Sophie
looked out the kitchen window. It was
cloudy *again*. But unlike yesterday,
when the sky had been filled with
thunderclouds, today the clouds were
light and fluffy like cotton. And, as
they watched, the sun shone through!

"The weather has cleared up—you can go out into the backyard!" Aunt Sophie said.

"Yay!" cried Ava and Oliver together. They whizzed up the stairs to find the Hatchimals, who were practicing their flying skills.

"Come on!" Oliver called to Pippi and Duke, grabbing his shoes. "We're going back to Hatchtopia!"

"Woo-hoo!" cheered the Hatchimals.

In less time than it would take a

A Cloudy Day

Hatchimal to loop the loop, Ava and Oliver had clattered back down the stairs with Duke and Pippi hidden safely inside their coat pockets.

"Where should we go in Hatchtopia?" Oliver asked.

The Frozen Wish

"The Wishing Star Waterfall, which makes your wishes come true!" called Ava, pushing open the back door. Duke had told them all about the waterfall last time they were in Hatchtopia.

"Or Lilac Lake, which turns you purple!" Oliver called back with a grin. As they made their way out into the yard, he slowed a little and lifted Duke out of his pocket. The Draggle's eyes were green—riding in Oliver's pocket had made him queasy! "What do you think, Duke?"

A Cloudy Day

Duke grinned. "Surprise!" he said.

"Pippi said that last night, too," Ava told Oliver. "What do you think they mean?"

"Let's get through to Hatchtopia. They can tell us there!" said Oliver. Ava and Oliver could understand the Hatchimals better when they were in their own world.

They reached the mighty magnolia tree that stood at the end of the yard, its leaves rustling in the breeze. Ava looked carefully at the trunk. She

The Frozen Wish

could still hardly believe
that this was where
the secret entrance
to Hatchtopia was
hidden!

Ava crouched
down and gently ran her hands
across the knobby tree trunk.

"Uh-oh," she said nervously.
"I think the doorway has vanished.
I can't see it at all!"

"Don't forget that the door won't
appear unless we tap on the tree trunk,"

A Cloudy Day

Oliver reminded her. "Otherwise everyone would know it was there, and then Hatchtopia would be full of journalists and it would be all over the news and all the grown-ups would know that Hatchimals are real." He shuddered. "Ugh."

"We'd better be quick," said Ava. "I think I saw Aunt Sophie watching us out the window!" She reached toward the tree and began to tap on the trunk. Oliver crouched down and joined in.

Tat- a-tat.

Tat- a-tat.

Tat- a-tat!

A faint outline appeared on the tree trunk. It shone more brightly, then the hidden door swung open.

Ava gasped. As the little door opened, she caught a glimpse of Hatchtopia in miniature, and the sight took her breath away. She'd almost forgotten how beautiful the

A Cloudy Day

Hatchimals' world was!
Slowly, carefully, she reached her
hand through the tiny doorway . . .

Something Peculiar

"Wheeeeeee!"

Ava had forgotten how odd it felt to shrink when she stepped through the tree trunk into Hatchtopia. It was like rushing down a magical slide. One minute, she was Ava-size; the next, she was only a little bigger than a Hatchimal. She couldn't wait to be almost the same size as Pippi again!

Oliver followed, then Duke and Pippi, before the door closed behind them with a soft thud.

"Whoa," murmured Ava.

Hatchtopia lay before them, as beautiful and as breathtaking as ever. Everything seemed bolder and brighter than in Ava and Oliver's world. The grass was a dazzling emerald green. The flowers were so vibrant, it was as if they'd been made from the colors of actual rainbows.

Something Peculiar

Hazy blue mountains glowed in the distance. Tall trees with glossy leaves stretched toward the sky.

The tree behind them gave a deep chuckle, which made everyone smile. This side of the doorway wasn't in a magnolia's trunk; it was in the Giggling Tree—the most important tree in all of Hatchtopia. The seed of every tree in the land came from the Giggling Tree.

"We're here at last!" exclaimed Ava. A bunch of friendly Hatchimals

came to greet them. Tigrette was
there, with his orange-and-black
stripes and silver wings, and so was
Ponette, a bright pink
creature with an
orange mane and
tail. There were
also many other
Hatchimals that the
children didn't recognize.

"Good morning!" said a green
Hatchimal. Her fur rose in soft
prickles, and she had claw-like feet

and small wings. "I'm Hedgyhen. You must be the humans I've heard so much about." She gave a small bow. "Have you come for the Glittering Garden Fireworks Fiesta?"

Ava's eyes widened.

Before she could answer, Pippi jumped in. "Yes, we have!" she said, putting one wing around Ava's waist. "We didn't want to say anything in case you were stuck

in the house again. But we so hoped you'd be able to come to Hatchtopia, because today's the Fireworks Fiesta. It's the most amazing fireworks display in all of Hatchtopia! The Glittering Garden Hatchimals organize it every year. All the fireworks look like beautiful flowers. It'll be a hundred times better than the fireworks display you missed."

"Wow!" said Ava. "Thank you, thank you, *thank you*!" She hugged Pippi, and behind them Oliver jumped up and down with excitement.

"Ah, your first visit to the fiesta is always special," Hedgyhen said with a smile. "Hatchimals come from far and . . ." Her voice trailed off. Something peculiar had happened.

A snowflake had landed on the end of her nose.

Ava, Oliver, Pippi, and Duke looked up at the sky. "It's snowing!" they cried.

"How magical!" said Ava.

"So cool!" said Oliver.

"What a disaster!" said Tigrette.

Something Peculiar

The children turned to the striped Hatchimal. He was pawing the ground and fluttering his wings with worry.

"It *never* snows in Giggle Grove or Glittering Garden!" he said. "It's always sunny. This is going to ruin the Fireworks Fiesta!"

The Frozen Wish

"The fireworks will be too soggy to light," Ponette said, tossing her mane fretfully.

Ava looked at their worried furry faces. She turned to Pippi. "If I went to Wishing Star Waterfall, could I wish the snow away?" she asked.

The Hatchimals oohed and aahed.

"That's a wonderful idea!" Ponette said. "But . . . you only have one chance to wish at Wishing Star Waterfall. We would hate for you to use up your one wish on us."

Something Peculiar

"It would be my pleasure," Ava said. And she really meant it. She was already so excited about the fireworks display, and she didn't want to miss it because of bad weather—she'd had enough of that back home!

Pippi gave Ava another big hug, and all the Hatchimals beamed at her.

"Let's go north to Wishing Star Waterfall!" said Duke, pointing the way.

The Frozen Wish

"It's not far—we'll be there in no time." He and Pippi took off at once, heading away from the Giggling Tree and zigzagging off through Giggle Grove.

Ava and Oliver waved goodbye to Tigrette, Ponette, and their new friend, Hedgyhen, then raced after their Hatchimals. As soon as they caught up, the children slowed to a brisk walk, and Duke and

Something Peculiar

Pippi flew beside them. New falling snowflakes whirled all around as they sped along.

"Phew!" said Ava, brushing her dark hair out of her eyes. "Hatchimal wings might be small, but they must be incredibly strong to make it so windy. No wonder you knocked over the Statue of Liberty model, Duke!"

Pippi nodded. "We need powerful wings to fly up to Cloud Cove," she said, circling around Ava and messing up her hair even more.

Something Peculiar

"Now I can't see a thing!" spluttered Ava, laughing. She reached up to tie her hair into a ponytail as Pippi giggled with delight and zoomed away.

The Hatchimals were soon flying so fast that Ava and Oliver had to run to keep up. Once they had left the bright woodland of Giggle Grove, they sped through Glittering Garden. The flowers sparkled and the grass twinkled an even brighter shade of green than in Giggle Grove, which Ava had hardly thought was possible.

43

The Frozen Wish

Enormous flowers caught snowflakes on their bright, silky petals, and Ava spotted little eggs tucked here and there among the stalks and leaves.

As they went, worried Hatchimals fluttered over to ask them what was going on. When the children reassured them that they were going to wish the snow away, the furry, feathery creatures looked very relieved!

*

Eventually, with tired legs and flushed

Something Peculiar

cheeks, Ava and Oliver arrived at the foot of the Wishing Star Waterfall. They took a moment to catch their breath, before looking up at the towering wall of water.

Then, as one, Ava and Oliver gasped.

"What happened?" asked Ava.

The Wishing Star Waterfall wasn't a waterfall.

It was a glacier.

Last time they'd been in Hatchtopia, thousands upon thousands of shooting stars had glittered and shone

as they tumbled down from high in the clouds. Now they hung motionless—a great, shining column of sparkles in the air. Even the pool below had turned to ice.

The cold weather had frozen the Wishing Star Waterfall!

All of a sudden there was a loud **crack**. Ava and Oliver looked down to see a furry creature breaking through the ice.

"Greetings!" The Hatchimal was blue, with the face of a sea lion. She spoke shyly as she shook icy droplets from her fur.

"You're a long way from home!" said Pippi. She turned to the others, adding, "Sealark comes from Polar Paradise, which is many wingbeats from here."

"I'm on vacation," said Sealark in a little voice. "I've come to see the Fireworks Fiesta."

Something Peculiar

"Hello!" said Oliver, with a bow. "We've come to wish away the snow. Ponette says the fireworks can't happen if it's wet."

"Glittering Garden seems a funny place to come if you're used to freezing temperatures," Duke said to Sealark. "Didn't you want to go somewhere icy on vacation?"

Now Sealark looked really uncomfortable.

"What's wrong?" asked Ava softly.

"I've done something terrible,"

whispered Sealark. "I've always wanted to come to the Fireworks Fiesta. But when I got here, it was far too hot for me. So I leaped into the Wishing Star Waterfall and wished for the weather to be colder. But no one else seems to be enjoying it. So I've tried to wish the snow away, but of course you're only allowed one wish, and now the waterfall has frozen and Glittering Garden is covered in snow, and I'm afraid I've ruined *everything*!"

The poor Polar Hatchimal bobbed

up and down anxiously in the icy water.

"Don't worry!" Ava said. "We'll make a wish and then Hatchtopia will be back to normal."

The Frozen Wish

"Everything will be all right," agreed Pippi. "And it'll be even more fun sliding down the waterfall when it's icy!"

Sealark seemed to cheer up a little. "Oh, thank you!" she said. "I'm so very sorry for all the trouble! Is there *anything* I can do to help?"

"We'll tell you if there is," Ava assured her.

"Thank you *so* much!" said Sealark. Then she flipped over to reveal a perfect blue tail and pink wings,

Something Peculiar

before plunging under the water and out of sight.

"How many different kinds of Hatchimal *are* there?" asked Ava.

Pippi laughed. "You wouldn't believe me if I told you," she said. "Let's just say there are *a lot*."

"Ahem," said Oliver, pointing upward. "Aren't we supposed to be wishing?"

Everyone looked up and up and up.

The Frozen Wish

The waterfall might have been frozen, but it was still beautiful. Its stars shone even brighter when suspended in ice. Thick white clouds were piled high above the waterfall like whipped cream.

"Let's fly you up there to make your wishes," Duke said.

"*Really?*" asked Ava. "You'll fly us up to Cloud Cove?"

"Well, how else are you going to get up there?" Pippi smiled at her friend.

"But how can you fly us up?" Oliver asked. "We can't ride on your backs—we're bigger than you are!"

Duke grinned and fluttered into the air, hovering just above Oliver's head. "Grab my feet!" he said.

Oliver looked at Ava, wide-eyed.

Ava shrugged. "It might work," she said. "Try it!"

Looking more than a little nervous, Oliver reached up and caught hold of his Hatchimal's blue feet.

"Ready?" said Duke.

Oliver nodded.

"Then let's go!" said the Draggle.

Up, Up, and Away

Ava watched in astonishment as Duke rose slowly upward, pulling Oliver up until his feet lifted off the ground.

Next, it was Ava's turn. She smiled nervously at Pippi, who was fluttering above her. Then Ava held on tight and tried not to squeak as the Penguala lifted her up into the air.

Whoosh!

They were off, soaring high up the wall of ice. Then, just as Ava's arms were growing tired, the Hatchimals rose above the lip of the waterfall, and Cloud Cove was revealed in all its wonderfulness.

The Frozen Wish

"Wow," breathed Ava as they hovered in the air.

A glassy lake lay below them, but it was unlike any lake Ava had ever seen before. At its edges, there were no grassy banks or stony shores. Instead, the pool of water nestled among rolling clouds. And, just like the waterfall, it was frozen solid.

Gracefully, the Hatchimals swooped downward to allow the children to land softly on the misty banks of the cove. They glided down to stand beside them.

Something Peculiar

"Welcome to Cloud Cove!" said Duke proudly. "It's not usually this icy . . . but what do you think of the place?"

"It's like a gigantic comforter!" said Oliver, bouncing gently on the white cloud.

"It reminds me of marshmallows," said Ava. She poked her finger into the cloud, then stuck it in her mouth. "But it doesn't *taste* like marshmallows."

She pulled a face. "It's just like water."

"Clouds in Hatchtopia are like clouds in your world," explained Pippi. "They're made of tiny droplets of water that are so light they float in the air. But the clouds of Cloud Cove are extra special, which is why you can stand on them! When we fly up here, our coats become extra soft."

Ava sighed happily. "It's beautiful," she said, her breath making icy puffs in the cold air.

Something Peculiar

Duke nudged Oliver. "Ava's going to wish for warm weather, but have you decided what to wish for?" the Draggle asked.

Oliver smiled and nodded. "I made up my mind as soon as we got here," he said. "But I want it to be a surprise!"

"Excellent," said Duke. "Now, if everyone's ready, we might as well skate across the lake. It's solid ice!"

Together, Ava, Oliver, and their Hatchimals glided across the ice. Their feet left swirling patterns as they went.

The Frozen Wish

"Isn't this amazing?" cried Ava, spinning on the spot.

"Er, yes . . . ," said Oliver, who was somehow going backward.

Everyone slid to a halt at the top of the waterfall—except for Oliver, who collapsed in a heap.

The Frozen Wish

"Let's go!" said Pippi, flapping her wings and rising gently into the air. "You jump, then we'll fly down beside you and whisk you away before you reach the bottom. Usually, wishers splash into the water, but right now it would be a hard landing on the ice!"

Ava took a deep breath, and then, on the count of three, she slid over the edge of the frozen waterfall. Down, down, down she plummeted. She went so fast down the icy-cold slide that her hair streamed out behind her,

Something Peculiar

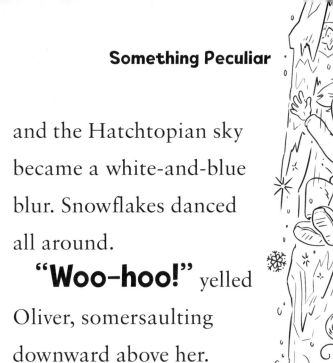

and the Hatchtopian sky became a white-and-blue blur. Snowflakes danced all around.

"Woo-hoo!" yelled Oliver, somersaulting downward above her.

"Wheeeee!" called Duke and Pippi,

rocketing past on the right.

"I wish that the weather would go back to how it should be!" Ava whispered to the Wishing Star Waterfall as she fell.

At the very last minute, the Hatchimals swooped beneath Ava and Oliver. The kids hung on tightly to the Hatchimals' feet as the creatures set them down gently near the bottom of the waterfall.

"I made my wish!" said Ava. She was shaking with cold after her icy tumble and she wished she could have made *two* wishes—then she could have asked for thick fur like Pippi's to keep her warm! As if reading her thoughts, the Penguala glided over and gave Ava a big fuzzy cuddle.

"What did you wish for, Ollie?" Ava asked, snuggling into Pippi's warm fur.

"If I tell you," Oliver said, shivering, "then it won't be a surprise." He laughed as Duke barreled him over in a furry hug.

Once he was warm again, Oliver

The Frozen Wish

sat up on the bank and frowned. "You *did* wish for the weather to go back to normal, didn't you, sis?" he asked.

Ava nodded. "I did."

They both turned their faces up to the sky. It still whirled with snowflakes. They landed on Ava's eyelashes, and she blinked them away sadly.

Something Peculiar

"It looks like your wish didn't come true," said Oliver.

"Did yours?" Ava asked.

"Not yet," Oliver told her, still looking up at the sky. He waited.

Ava resisted the urge to ask him again what he'd wished for.

"No," Oliver said at last, looking downcast. "My wish hasn't come true, either."

The children stared at each other in dismay. What had happened to Wishing Star Waterfall?

Missing Wishes

"The wishes aren't working!" Pippi said, her eyes a deep, dark blue. "Maybe it's because the waterfall is frozen . . . but why would that change anything? The wishing stars are still there. I can see them!"

"This is an emergency," said Oliver. "Something needs to be done *now*!"

The Frozen Wish

The Hatchimals turned to him with eager eyes.

"Can you help?" asked Duke.

"You'll figure out how to fix it, won't you?" Pippi said.

"Umm," Oliver muttered. "Ava, *say* something," he whispered. "Come on, you're the eldest. It's your job."

Ava rolled her eyes at him, but turned to the Hatchimals. "We'd love to help," she said, "but I'm afraid we don't have any experience with this sort of thing. Wishes aren't the same in our world, you see. They don't always work. We usually just cross our fingers and hope for the best."

"Oh dear," said Pippi, her face falling. "So you *can't* make the wishes come true? Then what are we going to do?"

"We'll help solve the problem, of course," Ava assured her. "If we can figure out *how*."

There was a gentle **splash**.

"This is all my fault," said a sorrowful voice.

The Frozen Wish

 It was Sealark, poking her head through the jagged hole in the ice that she'd made earlier. Her beautiful blue fur glistened with droplets. She leaped out of the hole in a perfect arc and slid to a halt beside them. Her nose twitched as a tear rolled down her cheek. "I've broken the Wishing Star Waterfall. I'll never forgive myself!"

Missing Wishes

Pippi patted her shoulder gently. "Don't worry," she said. "We'll find the answer. We just need to figure out who to ask."

"Oh, I know who you can ask," said Sealark, sniffling.

"Who?" asked Oliver.

"Swotter," said Sealark. "She's probably the wisest creature in all of Hatchtopia. I'm sure she'll be able to tell you everything you need to know."

"Awesome!" said Oliver. "But . . . where do we find her?"

The Frozen Wish

In their own world, he and Ava could have searched for the information online, but he guessed there was nothing like the Internet in Hatchtopia. And he hadn't seen a library anywhere.

Thankfully, Sealark knew the answer to this, too. "Well, she's from the River family. So the river will be the best place to find her!"

"Thanks, Sealark!" said Oliver.

"Hang on!" Duke said to Oliver, flying up to head height and waggling

his feet. "We'll get to the river faster if we fly. There's no time to waste when the future of the Wishing Star Waterfall is at stake."

"Not to mention the Fireworks Fiesta!" Ava exclaimed as she and Pippi launched into the air alongside Oliver and Duke.

"I'll guide you to Swotter," called Sealark. She jumped back through the hole in the ice, and swam off down the frozen brook that curved away from the waterfall. The others could see her pink wings sparkling beneath the surface of the glassy ice.

And then, in a sudden flutter of bright Hatchimals' wings, they were off!

"The river flows between Giggle Grove and Glittering Garden, then on to the Ocean of Hatchtopia," Pippi told Ava and Oliver. "Keep your eyes on Sealark!"

Duke and Pippi flew low above the frozen water, following the shining brook's path through Hatchtopia.

The Frozen Wish

The stream grew wider and wider,
until it became a mighty frozen
river.

Ava was so busy keeping her eyes
on Sealark that she only spotted the
wooden footbridge at the very last
moment.

Missing Wishes

"Whoa!" she yelled, just as both Hatchimals dived downward and flew under the bridge. It was a tight fit, with less than an inch to spare above them. Everything went dark for a second and then—**bam!**—they were back in the daylight again, flying much lower now and skimming the river's icy surface.

"That was Blushing Bridge," explained Pippi, puffing slightly. "It was built by the Giggle Grove and Glittering Garden Hatchimals to join their lands!"

The Frozen Wish

"Right!" said Ava, her heart still thumping from the sudden dive. "That was an interesting surprise!"

She could see Glittering Garden in the distance now. It had been completely transformed by the falling snow. As they drew closer, Ava saw that the enormous daisies had closed up, retreating from the cold. The grass was crisp with frost, and the brightly colored flowers were muted to soft pastel shades under the dusting of sparkling snow.

Missing Wishes

"Swotter should be somewhere near here," said Pippi, looking down.

Beneath the ice, the river water shone a deep turquoise blue, which made it difficult to keep their eyes on Sealark. They heard a cracking sound, and saw Sealark's head bob up through a hole in the ice. She was pointing a wing in the direction of some reeds on the banks of Glittering Garden.

"There she is!" Sealark called.

The Frozen Wish

As Pippi and Duke landed, setting Ava and Oliver down on the shore, a Hatchimal poked her head out from among the reeds.

Swotter was a dark pink-red color, with bright green scales on her tummy.

Missing Wishes

Sealark darted away up the river, and Ava wondered if she was still feeling embarrassed about her wish. It seemed better to let her go and reassure her later.

"Yes . . . ?" asked Swotter. Her voice was deep and melodic, like the low notes of a piano.

"Um, hello!" said Ava nervously. "We'd like to ask you some questions, if we may."

"I thought you might say that," said Swotter, gazing up at them.

The Frozen Wish

Ava stared back, mesmerized. It was impossible to tell the color of Swotter's eyes. Different shades swirled and whirled in them, making Ava feel quite dizzy.

"*Everyone* asks me questions," Swotter continued. "The question is, which question will *you* ask?"

Ava shifted from one foot to the other, the snow crunching beneath her shoes. Talking to Swotter made her feel a bit nervous. "The Wishing Star Waterfall has stopped granting wishes," she said. "But we don't know why. So we thought if I asked you how the waterfall works, then we could maybe figure out why it isn't working now. Can you tell us? Please?"

"Hmmmm," said Swotter, in a mysterious sort of way.

The Hatchimal was silent for so long that Ava started to worry that she hadn't heard the question. Then suddenly Swotter looked right at Ava and spoke.

"Usually, we only see shooting stars

when they blaze through the night,"
murmured Swotter. "But some are
caught in the waterfall as they shoot
across the sky. Anyone who slides
down Wishing Star Waterfall for the
very first time can make a wish, and
that wish will come true."

"I made a wish when I slid down
the waterfall," Ava said, "but it didn't
come true. Do you know why? Is it
because the waterfall is frozen?"

Swotter nodded. "Indeed," she said.
"Think carefully. What sort of stars

do you wish upon?"

Ava thought hard. "Shooting stars?" she suggested.

Swotter smiled slowly. "Yes. The stars must be moving for the wishes to come true. You cannot wish upon a star that's frozen in place. Why, that would be no better than wishing on a dandelion!" she said.

"Oh no!" cried Oliver. "If the stars stay frozen, there will never be any more wishes!" He turned to Ava. "What are we going to do?!"

A Cloudy Problem

Ava gasped. "I've got it!"

"*What* have you got?" demanded Oliver.

"We need to make the waterfall move again—and it'll move if it's not frozen!" Ava exclaimed. "So we need to *defrost* it."

Oliver's eyes widened until they

were almost as big as Duke's.

"Brilliant!" he breathed. "But . . . how do we do that?"

"There's nothing big enough or hot enough in Hatchtopia to melt a whole waterfall!" Pippi said, looking worried.

"What keeps everyone warm in Hatchtopia?" Swotter asked.

"The sun!" said Ava.

"Exactly," said Swotter.

"But the clouds are blocking the sun . . . ," Ava said slowly. She turned

A Cloudy Problem

to her brother. "Ollie, do you remember what happened at home when the clouds cleared?"

"It got warmer!" exclaimed Oliver.

They all looked up at the thick cloud above Glittering Garden. The sky had been just as cloudy in Cloud Cove, above the waterfall.

"Do you think that maybe, above the clouds, the sun is still shining?" Duke asked.

"I'll go and check it out," said Pippi. "It's higher than I've ever been before, but I think I can make it." She gulped.

"Good luck!" everyone shouted as the brave Penguala galloped along the ground, then launched herself into the air. Her multicolored wings pumped up and down, faster and faster, powering her skyward through the falling snow. It wasn't long before Pippi disappeared into the clouds above.

The Frozen Wish

"Is she almost there?" said Oliver, squinting up at the sky. "Oh, I wish we could see her."

"Actually," said Ava, "I think she's on her way back!"

A tiny dot appeared, then grew

until it was a dark smudge, and then a Hatchimal-shaped silhouette. At last, they could see that it was definitely Pippi, who touched down with a weary **"Oof!"**

"It's true," the Penguala panted, her breath misting in the cold air. "Up above the clouds, the sun is shining, just like normal!"

"Right," said Oliver in a determined voice. He rubbed his hands together. "So, now that we know what's happening, what do we do next?"

99

The Frozen Wish

Duke and Pippi stared up at Ava. Even Swotter was looking expectantly at her.

Oh dear. Not a single idea popped into Ava's head. She stared back at them all, wondering if this was what it felt like to be a goldfish in a bowl, with everyone gawking through the glass. "Can't you think of any ideas, Swotter?" she asked hopefully.

"I'm afraid not," replied the wise Hatchimal. "But . . . maybe you should look for a solution that brings everyone together."

That sounded like a riddle, and it didn't help much.

Hmm. Ava looked around for inspiration. Nothing sprang to mind. Maybe if she acted as though she were thinking deeply, then she really would come up with something clever . . .

So she rubbed her chin thoughtfully.

She shut her eyes and pressed her fingers to her forehead.

She marched around in a circle.

She made a serious face.

The Frozen Wish

She snapped her fingers.

In despair, she flopped to the frosty ground and stared up at the sky, wiping away snowflakes as they melted on her cheeks. Even more white clouds were rolling toward Wishing Star Waterfall, blown by a faraway breeze.

Then, all of a sudden, Ava knew exactly what to do.

"Pippi," she said, springing to her feet, "is there a way of summoning the Hatchimals? We're going to need to get as many of you together as possible."

A Cloudy Problem

The Penguala stood up straight. "Of course," she said. "I can ring the bluebell flower in the schoolhouse.

That's the school bell—it sounds at the beginning and end of lessons. But if it rings at any other time of the day, then all the Hatchimals know there's an emergency and they'll come at once."

"It's *incredibly* loud," Duke added.

"Excellent!" said Ava. "That's just what we need!"

While they were speaking, Oliver had been hopping impatiently from one foot to the other, kicking up snow. As soon as there was the tiniest pause, he said, "So, what's the plan?"

A Cloudy Problem

"Remember how the wind from Duke's wings knocked over the figurine of the Statue of Liberty? And how Pippi and Duke flew around us in circles and blew my hair all over the place?" said Ava.

Oliver nodded. "That's why it's even messier than usual."

Ava laughed. "Exactly. So, if that's how breezy it is when just one or two Hatchimals are flying," she went on, "imagine how windy it will become when there's a whole crowd

of Hatchimals! If you all fly around
in circles, then perhaps you can make
enough wind to blow all the clouds
away. And then the sun will be able to
warm up Wishing Star Waterfall again!"

"Genius!" cried Oliver. He gave Ava
a high five.

"That's a hatchtastic idea!" the
Penguala added, swooping around the
giant snowy daisies. Then she half ran,
half flew to the schoolhouse, where
she pushed the enormous bluebell to
and fro.

A Cloudy Problem

Ding! Dang! Dong!

Duke was right. The bluebell was incredibly loud. So loud it made the ground wobble.

But it worked. Within a few seconds, Hatchimals started fluttering into Glittering Garden. Tigrette and Ponette were among the first, their manes dusted with icy flakes. Then Kittycan arrived, swiftly followed by Koalabee, Elefly, and Bunwee. Soon there were so many of them that no one could see the snow-covered flowers.

When the number of Hatchimals had climbed past fifty, Ava stood on Blushing Bridge to explain her plan to them all. They listened carefully, and she was relieved to see a ripple flow across the rainbow crowd as everyone nodded their approval.

"It's a *wonderful* idea," said Tigrette. "But why *is* it so snowy and cloudy? That's what I'd like to know."

At the very back, Ava spotted Sealark, who was blushing guiltily.

Sealark took a step forward, paused, and then seemed to make up her mind. "It was my first visit to this part of Hatchtopia," she said. "It was so warm! So"—she gulped—"I wished for it to be colder. I never expected it to get *so* very cold, or to upset everybody else. I'm so sorry!"

There was a hushed pause. And then a lilac giraffe-like creature beside

The Frozen Wish

Sealark patted her on the back. "Well, I once wished for a purple lake," she said with a smile. "We've all made mistakes—and everything always

turns out all right in the end!"

Ava beamed at the Hatchimals.
She'd known they would forgive
Sealark.

"So," Ava said, "will you try to blow the clouds away?"

"Of course!" cried Ponette. "Will you be coming with us?"

Ava took a deep breath. "I'd like to," she said.

"And so would I!" added Oliver, who was now stretching his muscles the way he'd seen runners do before a race.

"Then we'd be delighted to take you," said Duke, flying forward with Pippi.

Oliver whooped with delight,

grabbing Duke's feet before the Draggle was quite ready. Duke laughed and beat his wings to steady himself. He soon recovered—and told his passenger to hold on tight.

"Ready, set, GO!" said Oliver.

Ava grabbed on to Pippi's feet, too. "The only way is up!" she said.

Wish Upon a Star

The crowd of Hatchimals rose
majestically into the air—a dazzling
array of color against the snowy white
world beneath them. They hovered
for a moment before swooping toward
the frozen Wishing Star Waterfall and
then up, up, up into the air.

Ava felt the wind whipping past her.

She held
on tightly to
Pippi's feet as
they flew faster
and faster. Soon
they were higher
than Cloud Cove,
and the blanket of
cloud hung in the sky just
above them. The air whirled
with glittering snowflakes. It was
like being inside a giant snow globe.
"Attention, everyone!"

Ava cried. "Let's blow these clouds out of the sky!"

There was a huge cheer from the Hatchimals.

"Can I go first?" Sealark said quietly to Ava. "I created this problem, so I'd like to help fix it, if I can."

Ava smiled. "Go for it!"

So Sealark led the way. She flew in a wide curve, and the rest of the Hatchimals followed, one after the other. Pippi and Duke went last, to complete the ring of whirling creatures that flew in circles like a giant merry-go-round.

The Hatchimals flew faster and faster and faster, until they were whizzing around so quickly, Ava found it impossible to tell one creature from another. The wind created by their

wings was so strong!

"Look!" Oliver gasped. The air caught his words, and Ava could hardly hear him. "Have we created a *tornado*?"

"Wow!" Ava stared in amazement. In the center of the Hatchimals' circle,

the wind was spinning the clouds into a huge swirling cone.

Whoosh!

The circle of Hatchimals began to slow down. For a few seconds nothing happened, and Ava realized that she was holding her breath. If she hadn't been holding on to Pippi's feet as well, she would have covered her eyes, because she hardly dared to watch.

All at once, the clouds spun away in a frothing wave . . . and the sun shone through!

"Yay!" cried Ava and Oliver. All the Hatchimals cheered. Sealark was the loudest of them all.

"It's practically summer already!" said Pippi.

She was right. The sun's soft rays were bathing everyone and everything in a wonderfully warm glow.

"Let's see if the waterfall is still frozen!" Ava shouted to Oliver.

Pippi and Duke swooped down, pulling Ava and Oliver back in the direction of Cloud Cove. As it loomed

larger, they saw that the ice was beginning to melt. The water in the cove was rippling gently against the soft, pillowy clouds as they landed.

Craaaaack!

With a sound so loud that it made the clouds tremble, the silvery ice was starting to thaw and break.

Wish Upon a Star

Ava spotted sparkling stars
flying free as chunks of ice tumbled
downward and the water began to
flow again.

"Quick!" Ava said. "Ollie, we need to
slide down the waterfall and make our
wishes again, now that it's working!"

Oliver didn't need to be told twice.
He raced over, grabbed Ava's hand,
and together they leaped into the
waterfall. Pippi and Duke swooped
down with them, batting any falling
ice away with their wings.

"I wish that the weather would go back to normal!" Ava cried. This time the stars danced through the water around her, and as she made her wish, they seemed to shine extra brightly.

Then . . . **Whoosh!** Pippi was there to catch her before she fell into the chilly water.

As Pippi and Duke flew them back up into Cloud Cove, Ava watched the last of the snowy clouds race back toward Polar Paradise, where they belonged.

Wish Upon a Star

"We did it!" she yelled as they landed.

Ava, Oliver, Pippi, and Duke hatch-fived and hugged one another. Then they settled down in the puffy clouds to enjoy the view. Soon other Hatchimals joined them, bringing picnic baskets filled with delicious snacks. Ava hadn't realized how hungry she was until she took a bite of some Friendship Farm fudge and sipped some sunny orange juice from Citrus Coast.

Night fell as the Hatchimals laughed and told stories up high in the clouds.

"What *did* you wish for, Ollie?" Ava asked, settling back into a pillowy cloud.

Boom! Bang! Pop! Pow!

Magnificent flashes filled the sky.

The sparkling lights formed the shapes of daisies and roses and hundreds of forget-me-nots, glittering for just a moment before they were replaced by new explosions.

"Fireworks!" yelled Oliver.

The Frozen Wish

"I wished that you would get to see the fireworks display!"

Ava was so happy that she couldn't say any more. Instead, she pulled her brother into a huge hug, then sat down beside him and watched the best fireworks display she'd seen in her life. And, up in Cloud Cove, they had the best view in Hatchtopia.

*

"I can't thank you enough," said Sealark later, as Ava and Oliver stood beside the Giggling Tree once more, ready to return home. "Next time, I won't be so silly. I'll think about other people before I make a wish!"

Ava patted the Hatchimal on the shoulder. "Don't worry. And we couldn't have fixed it without your help," she reminded Sealark.

"Besides, I do silly things all the time," said Oliver. To prove it, he ran up the Giggling Tree's trunk and tried to do a backflip, but landed flat on his back instead. "See?"

Sealark snorted with laughter

The Frozen Wish

and, once Ava had made sure that her brother was all right, she laughed, too.

Oliver pretended to be upset until the Giggling Tree started chuckling as well, and he couldn't keep a straight face any longer. They were all laughing so hard that nobody noticed Pippi and Duke each slipping something into the children's pockets.

And then, all too soon, it was time to go home.

*

Back in Ava and Oliver's world, it was still daytime. Time passed differently in Hatchtopia, which was perfect, because it made it so much easier to visit!

As Ava and Oliver headed into their house, Aunt Sophie greeted them at the door with a big smile.

"I thought your funny little creatures needed somewhere to sleep," she said. "So I made these."

"Cool!" said Oliver. "But, umm, what are they?"

"Are they Hatchimals' nests?" guessed Ava as she held one of the soft, cuddly nests. Aunt Sophie had made it from old scraps of material and strands of yarn. Around the edges, they were decorated with glittering stars.

"They are! I know I can be a little too serious sometimes," said Aunt Sophie, "but I've loved staying with you."

Ava and Oliver both hugged her.

"Thank you for looking after us," said Ava.

Wish Upon a Star

"And thank you for the nests!" said Oliver. "Duke and Pippi will love them."

Ava felt Pippi cooing in her pocket, and quietly shushed her. "You're a toy again, remember!" she whispered.

As Aunt Sophie headed into the kitchen, Ava put her hand in her other pocket and realized there was something inside it—something smooth and solid and pointy.

She pulled out a small shiny star and stared at it in amazement.

The Frozen Wish

She nudged Oliver and showed it to him, then pointed to his pocket.

Oliver pulled out a star, too!

"Shooting stars!" cooed Pippi in a tiny voice, poking her head out first to check that Aunt Sophie wasn't within earshot. "For you!"

Ava and Oliver were thrilled.

"They're beautiful!" Ava exclaimed. "And we can keep them?"

Pippi and Duke nodded, their eyes glowing pink.

"I'm going to stick it to my bedroom ceiling," Oliver declared. "Then it'll twinkle up there like a real star!"

Ava thought that was an amazing idea. That way, every night when she went to bed, she would be reminded of her friends in Hatchtopia.

THE END

Ava and Oliver loved their latest trip to Hatchtopia! But the magical adventures don't end when Ava and Oliver leave. Can you write your own short story about what happens next?

Use the questions to help you.

How does Sealark get home to Polar Paradise?

_____

_____

_____

_____

_____

_____

_____

_____

What's the next mystery that Swotter helps solve?

What wishes do the Hatchimals make, now that the waterfall is working again?

_____

_____

_____

_____

_____

Anyone who slides down Wishing Star Waterfall for the first time can make a wish, and it will come true! What would you wish for?

Choose carefully—you only get one wish!

_____

_____

_____

Also available